Written by Gaby Goldsack
Illustrated by Steve Smallman

This edition published by Parragon in 2008

Parragon
Queen Street House
4 Queen Street
Bath BA1 1HE, UK

ISBN 978-1-4075-3171-7

Tractor Trouble

Illustrated by Steve Smallman

Bath · New York · Singapore · Hong Kong · Cologne · Delhi · Melbourne

Farmer Fred was going to have a very busy day.

"Look at all these jobs that need doing," said his wife, Jenny, waving a long list.

"Don't worry!" said Farmer Fred. "With the tractor's help, I'll have them done before you can say *cauliflowers.*"

"Come on, Patch!" he said to his trusty sheepdog.

Farmer Fred sped off on his tractor. The first job was to plow Top Field.

"Woof! Woof!" barked Patch as the tractor whizzed past at high speed. The tractor was going too fast!

In the next field, Harry Horse trotted over to see what the noise was about.

He stuck his head over the hedge just as the tractor rushed past. The tractor tires sent mud spraying everywhere.

"Neigh!" cried Harry, as he was splattered with lumps of sticky mud.

But Farmer Fred didn't hear. He was already on his way to his next job.

In no time at all, Farmer Fred had hitched up the trailer of hay to the tractor.

"We'll have those cows fed before you can say *dandelions*," smiled Farmer Fred.

Farmer Fred rushed across Cowslip Meadow. The hay bales bounced this way and that. Patch raced after them.

"Woof! Woof!" barked Patch. The hay bales didn't look safe. But it was too late. A hay bale bounced off the trailer towards Connie Cow.

"Moo!" cried poor Connie as she ran into the creek.

"We've finished all our jobs in record time!" said Farmer Fred as he arrived in the barnyard. "Now, where is everyone?"

Farmer Fred looked around the yard, but he couldn't see any of the animals.

Just then, Patch came running into the yard. "Woof! Woof!" he barked.

"What is it, Patch?" asked Farmer Fred, puzzled. "Do you know where everyone has gone?"

Farmer Fred followed Patch out of the yard.

Harry Horse, Polly Pig, Shirley Sheep, and Hetty Hen were standing beside the creek.

Farmer Fred couldn't believe his eyes when he saw Connie Cow stuck in the brook.

"Blithering beets!" Farmer Fred gasped. "How did you get in there?"

"Moo!" said Connie Cow crossly.

"Never fear," said Farmer Fred, cheerfully. "I've an idea!"

Farmer Fred disappeared into the workshop. One by one, the animals gathered around to listen to the tapping and hissing noises coming from inside.

"Oh dear," clucked Hetty Hen. "What can Farmer Fred be making this time?"

"I just hope poor Connie is rescued soon," said Polly Pig. "You know how her milk curdles when she's upset!"

Just then, the door to the shed flew open and out came Farmer Fred, dragging...

"...The Inflatable Cow-floater," said Farmer Fred proudly. And off he bumped toward the creek.

Harry Horse and the others followed at a safe distance.

Within minutes, Farmer Fred had launched his Inflatable Cow-floater and was busy telling Connie Cow to climb aboard.

The animals held their breath as
Connie Cow wibbled and wobbled
on top of the Inflatable Cow-floater.

Slowly, Connie Cow floated off.
Then there was a scraping sound
and a loud hiss.

Connie Cow and the Inflatable Cow-floater sank back into the water.

"Patch," clucked Hetty Hen. "We have to rescue poor Connie."

"I'd pull her out myself, but..." sighed Harry Horse, "...I'm not as young as I was."

"The tractor is the only one who can help her now," Polly Pig grunted.

"Patch, you'll have to tell Farmer Fred," Shirley Sheep bleated. "He always listens to you!"

Patch ran off to the tractor.

"Woof, woof!" he barked as he jumped on the tractor.

"What's up, Patch?" asked Farmer Fred, scratching his head. "I haven't got time to drive the tractor now. I've got to think of a way to repair my Inflatable Cow-floater."

"Woof, woof!" barked Patch, picking up the rope attached to the back of the tractor.

"That's it! I've an even better idea!" shouted Farmer Fred. "I know just how to rescue Connie."

Farmer Fred drove the tractor down to the edge of the creek. He tied the rope to the Cow-floater.

"I don't think I can watch," clucked Hetty Hen, hiding her eyes.

"Poor Connie," mumbled Harry Horse, shaking his mud-splattered head.

Slowly and carefully, Farmer Fred pulled the tractor out of the creek. At last, Connie Cow was safe on dry land. All the animals cheered.

Neigh!

Oink!

Cluck!

Baa!

Later, in the barnyard, Farmer Fred was feeling very pleased with himself.

"Look!" he said, showing Jenny the list all ticked off, "I've finished all the jobs...

"...and thanks to the tractor, I've had time to clean Harry and rescue Connie!"

Jenny looked at Patch and smiled.